William Ewart Gladstone

Bulgarian Horrors and the Question of the East

William Ewart Gladstone

Bulgarian Horrors and the Question of the East

ISBN/EAN: 9783337412159

Printed in Europe, USA, Canada, Australia, Japan

Cover: Foto ©Andreas Hilbeck / pixelio.de

More available books at **www.hansebooks.com**

BULGARIAN HORRORS

AND THE

QUESTION OF THE EAST.

BY THE

RIGHT HON. W. E. GLADSTONE, M.P.

LONDON:
JOHN MURRAY, ALBEMARLE STREET.
1876.

LONDON:

PRINTED BY WILLIAM CLOWES AND SONS,
STAMFORD STREET AND CHARING CROSS.

B 2

CONTENTS.

—◆◆—

BULGARIAN HORRORS

AND THE

QUESTION OF THE EAST.

In the difficult question of the East, entangled by so
many cross-purposes and interests, the people of this
country have shown a just, but a very remarkable,
disposition to repose confidence in the Government
of the day : and the Government of the day has
availed itself to the uttermost of that disposition.
For months the nation was content, though measures
and communications known to be of the highest interest were in progress, to remain without official
information, and to subsist upon the fragmentary and
uncertain notices which alone would transpire through
the press. It had to dispense not only with official
information, but with discussion in the House of
Commons. Only on the thirty-first of July did the
House of Commons receive, from the bounty of the
Government, after interminable delays and in the
dregs of the Session, a single night in which to re-
view the transactions of the Administration, together

with those of other Powers, during a twelvemonth,
and to ascertain the prospects and policy of the
coming recess. The lateness of the period fixed for
the debate went far to insure its inefficiency. But
this was not enough; and further precautions were
adopted. It was announced that, if the debate over-
flowed this narrow limit, it could only be finished in
fragments; the ordinary business of the Government
must proceed in preference to it, but it could doubt-
less be renewed on some day of yet thinner benches,
deeper exhaustion, and greater nearness to the Twelfth
of August, the principal and inviolate festival of the
sportsman's calendar.

So much for discussion. Next as to information.
For not weeks only but months together, appeal after
appeal was made to the Government to supply Parliament with full and authentic information, in lieu of
the scanty and uncertain notices which alone could be
obtained from unofficial sources. Appeal after appeal
was met with dilatory pleas. In these pleas, taken
singly, there may often be much reason; but, in the
aggregate, they were pushed to excess. Some measure
was in progress, and could not be explained till it
was completed; or was completed, and therefore a
thing of the past, which had disappeared from the range
of discussion; or was in contemplation, and the public
interest would suffer by disclosure. During this
time, instead of preparing the papers and documents,
to be ready for instant presentation, when presenta-

tion might be allowable, they were left unprepared, so that after every reason and every pretext for withholding them had been exhausted, precious weeks were lost afresh in the necessary labours for, and of, the press.

And the ending of this extraordinary confidence on the one side, and of these free drafts upon it from the other, what has it been? That we have had by degrees, from private and voluntary exertion, the knowledge which it was the bounden duty of the Administration to supply : and that, by the light which this knowledge casts upon past events we learn with astonishment and horror that, so far as appears, we have been involved, in some amount, at least, of moral complicity with the basest and blackest outrages upon record within the present century, if not within the memory of man.

The effect of the course which was taken by the Government was by no means confined within the walls of Parliament. For securing the escape of a great question from public vigilance there is no expedient comparable to adjourning Parliamentary discussion of it until the dying hours of a Session. For thus it is brought before the public mind at a time when the nation is in holiday, when society as well as Parliament is prorogued, when the natural leaders of every country or municipal community are dispersed. It is the great vacation of the year, when no one expects, and few will consent, to be called to serious business. All, who are acquainted with the inner

working of our Parliamentary as well as our social
system, know the weight as well as the truth of what
I now say.

The state of the case, then, is this. The House of
Commons has in the main been ousted from that
legitimate share of influence which I may call its
jurisdiction in the case. A subject of paramount
weight goes before the people at the time when
the classes having leisure, and usually contributing
most to form and guide public opinion, are scattered, as disjointed units, over the face of this
and of other countries. In default of Parliamentary
action, and a public concentrated as usual, we must
proceed as we can, with impaired means of appeal.
But honour, duty, compassion, and I must add shame,
are sentiments never in a state of *coma*. The
working men of the country, whose condition is less
affected than that of others by the season, have to
their honour led the way, and shown that the great
heart of Britain has not ceased to beat. And the
large towns and cities, now following in troops, are
echoing back, each from its own place, the mingled
notes of horror, pain, and indignation.

Let them understand that the importance of their
meetings, on this occasion at least, cannot be over-
rated. As Inkerman was the soldiers' battle, so this
is the nation's crisis. The question is not only
whether unexampled wrongs shall receive effectual and
righteous condemnation, but whether the only effec-
tive security shall be taken against its repetition. In

order to take this security, the nation will have to speak through its Government: but we now see clearly that it must first teach its Government, almost as it would teach a lisping child, what to say. *Then* will be taken out of the way of an united Europe the sole efficient obstacle to the punishment of a gigantic wrong.

I have thus far endeavoured to describe how it has come about that the nation, deprived of its most rightful and most constitutional aids, has been called upon at the season when the task would under ordinary circumstances be impossible, to choose between leaving its most sacred duties unperformed, and taking the performance of them primarily into its own hands.

Had the call upon the country been only that of Servia, Bosnia, and the Herzegovina, it would have been a grave one. But it is now graver far. By a slow and difficult process, the details of which I shall presently consider, and through the aid partly of newspaper correspondence, and partly of the authorised agent of a foreign State, but not through our own Parliament, or Administration, or establishments abroad, we now know in détail that there have been perpetrated, under the immediate authority of a Government to which all the time we have been giving the strongest moral, and for part of the time even material support, crimes and outrages, so vast in scale as to exceed all modern example, and so unutterably vile as well as fierce in character, that it

passes the power of heart to conceive, and of tongue
and pen adequately to describe them. These are the
Bulgarian horrors; and the question is, What can
and should be done, either to punish, or to brand, or
to prevent?

The details of these abominations may be read
in published Reports, now known to be accurate
in the main. They are hardly fit for reproduc-
tion. The authors of the crimes are the agents,
the trusted, and in some instances, the since-pro-
moted servants,* of the Turkish Government. The
moral and material support, which during the year
has been afforded to the Turkish Government, has
been given by the Government of England on behalf
of the people of England. In order to a full compre-
hension of the practical question at issue, it will be
necessary to describe the true character and position
of the Turkish Power, and the policy, as I think it
the questionable and erroneous policy, of the British
Administration.

Let me endeavour very briefly to sketch, in the
rudest outline, what the Turkish race was and what
it is. It is not a question of Mahometanism simply,
but of Mahometanism compounded with the peculiar
character of a race. They are not the mild Ma-
hometans of India, nor the chivalrous Saladins of
Syria, nor the cultured Moors of Spain. They were,

---

* Of these there are named Ahmed Aga and Tussum Bey (Mr.
Schuyler); also Chevket Pacha (Consul Reade). Papers 5, p. 18.

upon the whole, from the black day when they first entered Europe, the one great anti-human specimen of humanity. Wherever they went, a broad line of blood marked the track behind them; and, as far as their dominion reached, civilisation disappeared from view. They represented everywhere government by force, as opposed to government by law. For the guide of this life they had a relentless fatalism : for its reward hereafter, a sensual paradise.

They were indeed a tremendous incarnation of military power. This advancing curse menaced the whole of Europe. It was only stayed, and that not in one generation, but in many, by the heroism of the European population of those very countries, part of which form at this moment the scene of war, and the anxious subject of diplomatic action. In the olden time, all Western Christendom sympathised with the resistance to the common enemy; and even during the hot and fierce struggles of the Reformation, there were prayers, if I mistake not, offered up in the English churches for the success of the Emperor, the head of the Roman Catholic power and influence, in his struggles with the Turk.

But although the Turk represented force as opposed to law, yet not even a government of force can be maintained without the aid of an intellectual element, such as he did not possess. Hence there grew up, what has been rare in the history of the world, a kind of tolerance in the midst of cruelty, tyranny, and rapine. Much of Christian life was contemptuously let alone ; much of the subordinate functions of government was allowed to devolve upon the bishops ; and a race of Greeks was attracted to Constantinople, which has all along made up, in some degree, the deficiencies of Turkish Islam in the element of mind, and which at this moment provides the Porte with its long known, and, I must add, highly esteemed Ambassador in London. Then there have been from time to time, but rarely, statesmen whom we have been too ready to mistake for specimens of what Turkey might become, whereas they were in truth more like *lusus naturæ*, on the favourable side ; monsters, so to speak, of virtue or intelligence ; and there were (and are) also, scattered through the community, men who were not indeed real citizens, but yet who have exhibited the true civic virtues, and who would have been citizens had there been a true polity around them. Besides all this, the conduct of the race has gradually been brought more under the eye of an Europe, which it has lost its power to resist or to defy ; and its central government, in conforming perforce to many of the forms and traditions of civilisation, has occasionally caught something of their spirit.

This, I think, is not an untrue description of the past, or even of the present. The decay of martial energy, in a Power which was for centuries the terror of the world, is wonderful. Of the two hundred millions sterling which in twenty years it borrowed from the credulity of European Exchanges,

a large part has been spent upon its military and
naval establishments. (The result is before us.) It is
at war with Servia, which has a population, I think,
under a million and a half, and an army which is
variously stated at from five to eight thousand; the
rest of those bearing arms are a hitherto half-drilled
militia. It is also at war with the few scores of
thousands of that very martial people, who inhabit
the mountain tract of Montenegro. Upon these
handfuls of our race, an empire of more than thirty
millions discharges all its might: for this purpose it
applies all it own resources, and the whole of the
property of its creditors; and, after two months of
desperate activity, it greatly plumes itself upon
having incompletely succeeded against Servia, and
less doubtfully failed against Montenegro. Shades
of Bajazets, Amuraths, and Mahmouds!

Twenty years ago, France and England determined to try a great experiment in remodelling the
administrative system of Turkey, with the hope of
curing its intolerable vices, and of making good its
not less intolerable deficiencies. For this purpose,
having defended her integrity, they made also her
independence secure; and they devised at Constantinople the reforms, which were publicly enacted in an
Imperial Firman or Hatti-humayoum. The successes
of the Crimean War, purchased (with the aid of Sar-
dinia) by a vast expenditure of French and English
life and treasure, gave to Turkey, for the first time

perhaps in her blood-stained history, twenty years of a repose not disturbed either by herself or by any foreign Power. The Cretan insurrection imparted a shock to confidence; but it was composed, and Turkey again was trusted. The insurrections of 1875, much more thoroughly examined, have disclosed the total failure of the Porte to fulfil the engagements, which she had contracted under circumstances peculiarly binding on interest, on honour, and on gratitude. Even these miserable insurrections, she had not the ability to put down. In the midway of the current events, a lurid glare is thrown over the whole case by the Bulgarian horrors. The knowledge of these events is, whether by indifference or bungling, kept back from us, but only for a time. The proofs are now sufficiently before us. And the case is this. Turkey, which stood only upon force, has in the main lost that force. It is a Prussian, we learn, who has planned her campaign. Power is gone, and the virtues, such as they are, of power; nothing but its passions and its pride remain.

It is time, then, to clear an account which we have long, perhaps too long, left unsettled, and almost unexamined.

In the discussion of this great and sad subject, the attitude and the proceedings of the British Government cannot possibly be left out of view. Indeed, the topic is, from the nature of the case, so prominent, and from the acts done, so peculiar, that I could hardly be excused from stating in express and decided terms what appear to me its grave errors; were it only that I may not seem, by an apparent reserve, also to insinuate against them a purposed complicity in crime, which it would be not only rash, but even wicked, to impute. The consequences of their acts have been, in my view, deplorable. But as respects the acts themselves, and the motives they appear to indicate, the faults I find are these. They have not understood the rights and duties, in regard to the subjects, and particularly the Christian subjects, of Turkey, which inseparably attach to this country in consequence of the Crimean War, and of the Treaty of Paris in 1856. They have been remiss when they ought to have been active; namely, in efforts to compose the Eastern revolts, by making provision against the terrible misgovernment which provoked them. They have been active, where they ought to have been circumspect and guarded. It is a grave charge, which cannot be withheld, that they have given to a maritime measure of humane precaution the cha-. racter of a military demonstration in support of the Turkish Government. They have seemed to be moved too little by an intelligent appreciation of prior obligations, and of the broad and deep interests of humanity, and too much by a disposition to keep out of sight what was disagreeable and might be inconvenient, and to consult and flatter the public opinion of the day in its ordinary,

that is to say, its narrow, selfish, epicurean humour. I admit that, until a recent date, an opinion
widely prevailed, and perhaps was not confined to
any particular party, that this game had been
played with success and even brilliancy, and that,
amidst whatever mishaps and miscarriages elsewhere,
the Government stood high upon its foreign, that
is, its Eastern policy, in the approval of the
country.

Since that time, but two or three weeks have
elapsed. But a curtain opaque and dense, which
at the Prorogation had been lifted but a few inches
from the ground, has since then—from day to day—
been slowly rising. And what a scene it has disclosed! and where! Nearly four long months have
passed, during which there has been maintained in
this country, almost until now, an unnatural and
deadly calm. We now look backwards over this tract
of lethargy as over days of ease purchased by dis-
honour, the prolonged fascination of an evil dream.
A voice, an almost solitary voice, sounded indeed over
sea and land, in the month of June, to warn us of what
was going on. There was no want of ears disposed
to listen, when the tale told was of wholesale massacre
perpetrated by the authority of a Government to
which we had procured, in our living memory,
twenty years of grace; and to which, without inquiring how those years had been employed, we
had this year defied Europe in affording the strong

support of the British name. Nor was this all; for those wholesale massacres were declared to be complicated and set off with crimes, by the side of which the horror and infamy of massacre itself grew pale. But what then? These allegations came from a nameless, an irresponsible, newspaper correspondent. With the instinct of prudent Englishmen, startled Peers and Members of Parliament put question after question to the Government. The effect, the general sense of the answers was what I may call a moral, though not a verbal, denial. Whatever they were meant to produce, they did produce the result, not of belief qualified by a reserve for occasional error, but of disbelief qualified by a reserve for purely accidental truth. And this was the attitude which, conformably to general and needful rules, we could not do otherwise than assume. For what was the staple of those answers? They consisted of warnings against exaggeration; of general attenuations of the matter, as what must be expected to happen among savage races, with a different idea or code of morals from our own; of cynical remarks, such as that the allegations of lingering inflictions hardly could be true, since the Turkish taste was known to incline towards dispatch; of difficulties in deciding on which side lay the balance of crime and cruelty; of bold assurances that the insurgents were the aggressors, suggesting the reflection that the chief responsibility must rest on him who strikes the first blow; of acquittals of the Turkish armies and authorities in general, by suggesting that we were really dealing with a momentary outbreak of fanaticism among a handful of irregulars, gone by almost as soon as come; and, above all, at first with calm denials of knowledge. It was these denials of knowledge, which we believed to amount to a negative demonstration.

For we know that we had a well-manned Embassy at Constantinople, and a network of Consulates and Vice-Consulates, really discharging diplomatic duties, all over the provinces of European Turkey. That villages could be burned down by scores, and men, women, and children murdered, or worse than murdered, by thousands, in a Turkish province lying between the capital and the scene of the recent excitements, and that our Embassy and Consulates could know nothing of it?— The thing was impossible. It could not be. — So silence was obtained, and relief; and the well-oiled machinery of our luxurious, indifferent life worked smoothly on. There was a pressure of inquiry, but the door was each time quickly closed upon the question, as the stone lid used to be shut down, in the *Campo Santo* of Naples, upon the mass of human corpses that lay festering beneath.

But inquiry was to be made. And at this point I think the Government are to be charged with a serious offence. For inquiry, in these times, means the employment of the Telegraph. But I must here turn aside for a moment, in the endeavour to do an act of justice.

The first alarm respecting the Bulgarian outrages was, I believe, that sounded in the 'Daily News,' on the 23rd of June. I am sensible of the many services constantly rendered by free journalism to humanity, to freedom, and to justice. I do not undervalue the performances, on this occasion, of the 'Times,' the *Doyen* of the press in this country, and perhaps in the world, or of the 'Daily Telegraph;' and our other great organs. But of all these services, so far as my knowledge goes, that which has been rendered by the 'Daily News,' through its foreign correspondence on this occasion, has been the most weighty, I may say, the most splendid.* We are now informed (Parl. Papers No. 5, p. 6) that the accounts received by the German Government confirm its report. It is even possible that, but for the courage, determination, and ability of this single organ, we might, even at this moment, have remained in darkness, and Bulgarian wretchedness might have been without its best and brightest hope.

On the 26th of June, the Duke of Argyll, in the House of Lords, and Mr. Forster in the House of Commons, made anxious inquiries respecting the statements contained in a communication from the

---

* I believe it is understood that the gentleman who has fought this battle—for a battle it has been—with such courage, intelligence, and conscientious care, is Mr. Pears, of Constantinople, correspondent of the 'Daily News,' for Bulgaria.

correspondent of the ' Daily News,' which had been published in the paper of the 23rd, following a more general statement on the 10th. In order not to load these pages too heavily, as well as on other grounds, I shall cite or describe, in referring to these proceedings, chiefly the replies of the Head of the Government.

In answer, then, to Mr. Forster, Mr. Disraeli said, " We have no information in our possession which justifies the statements, to which the Right Hon. gentleman refers." The disturbances appeared to have been begun " by strangers, burning the villages without reference to religion or race." A war was carried on between " Bashi-Bazouks and Circassians," on one side, and " the invaders " on the other, and no doubt, " with great atrocity," much to be deplored. Since that time, measures had been adopted to stop these " Bashi-Bazouks and Circassians." " I will merely repeat," he concluded, " that the information *which we have at various times received* does not justify the statements made in the journal which he has named."*

I must add Lord Derby's concluding sentence :—

" *As the noble Duke has thought the evidence in this matter sufficient to justify him* in bringing the subject before the House, I will make further inquiry, and communicate the result to your Lordships."

There were reasons enough why others besides the

---

* ' Times,' June 27.

Duke of Argyll, should have thought the evidence sufficient to require some notice. For, in the statement of the 'Daily News,' there were contained these ominous words : *—

June 16.—"Even now it is openly asserted by the Turks, that England has determined to help the Government to put down the various insurrections. England, says a Turkish journal, will defend us against Russia, while we look after our rebels."

So much for the first attempt to throw light into these dark places.

On the 8th of July, the 'Daily News' inserted a second communication from its correspondent at Constantinople, confirming and extending the purport of the first. On the 10th, Mr. Forster renewed his inquiries. Mr. Disraeli stated, that there had not yet been time to receive any reply to the inquiries made. And this, though the Telegraph passes in a few hours, and the statement in question had appeared on the 23rd of June. Even now the only efficient instrument was not put in action, nor did this happen until July 14th;† and within five days after that date, a British agent was on his way to the bloody scene. It is absolutely necessary that Her Majesty's Government should explain why the Telegraph had

---

* Parl. Papers, Turkey, 1876. No. 3, p. 336.
† Papers No. 5, p. 1.

not at once been employed on the 26th or 27th of June.

But other parts of the First Minister's reply require notice. He hoped, " for the sake of human nature itself," that the statements were scarcely warranted. There had without doubt been atrocities in Bulgaria. This was a war " not carried on by regular troops, in this case not even by irregular troops, but by a sort of *posse comitatûs* of an armed population." " I doubt whether torture " . . . . " has been practised on a great scale among an historical people, who seldom have, I believe, resorted to torture, but generally terminate their connection with culprits in a more expeditious manner (laughter)." Every effort had been made, and would continue to be made, " to soften and mitigate as much as possible the terrible scenes that are now inevitably occurring." Atrocities, he believed, were " inevitable, when wars are carried on in certain countries, *and between certain races.*"*

Down to this date what we have to observe is—

First. The deplorable inefficiency of the arrangements of the Government for receiving information.

Secondly. The yet more deplorable tardiness of the means, adopted under Parliamentary pressure, for enlarging their store of knowledge.

---

* ' Times,' July 15.

Thirdly. The effect of the answers of the Prime Minister, from which it could not but be collected, by Parliament and the public,

a. That the responsibility lay in the first instance with certain "invaders of Bulgaria."

b. That the deplorable atrocities, which had occurred, were fairly divided, and were such as were incidental to wars "between certain *races.*" What could and did this mean, but between Circassians on the one side, and Bulgarians on the other? It now appears that the Circassians had but a very small share in the matter.

c. While the Bulgarians were thus loaded with an even share of responsibility for the "atrocities," we were given to understand that the Turkish Government, and its authorized agents, appeared to be no parties to them.

d. That the "scenes," that is, as is now demonstrated, the wholesale murders, rapes, tortures, burnings, and the whole devilish enginery of crime, "were to be mitigated and softened as much as possible."

I am concerned to subjoin the following declarations stated to have been made by Lord Derby to a Deputation on the 14th of July.

"He did not in the least doubt that there had been many acts of cruelty, and of wanton cruelty, committed *by the irregular troops of both sides* . . . It was not a case of lambs and wolves, but *of some savage races,* fighting in a peculiarly savage manner." *

This declaration is a gross wrong inadvertently done to the people of Bulgaria; and it ought to be withdrawn.

Again, on the 17th of July, Mr. Baxter revived the interrogatories. By this time, as we have seen, the Government had used the Telegraph, and they had ordered *on the* 15*th* a real and special inquiry from Constantinople. The subject could no longer be entirely trifled with. The Prime Minister made a lengthened statement, which occupies two columns of the 'Times.' The main portion of it was extracted from official reports, which are now before the world; and which did not in the smallest degree sustain either the doctrine of a fair division of the blame of inevitable atrocities, or an acquittal of the Turkish Government. But the Minister added matter of his own. What wonder was it, as to the Circassians, that "when their villages were burned and their farms ravaged," "they should take matters into their own hands, and endeavour to defend themselves?" "Scenes had occurred towards the end of May, and so on,"

---

* 'Times,' July 1.

" from which with our feelings "—what fine feelings
we have!—" we naturally recoil." " We were constantly communicating," "I will not say remon-
strating, with the Turkish Government," for "*the
Turkish Government was most anxious to be guided by
the advice of the British Ambassador.*" And still the
guilt was to stand as a fairly divided guilt.

" There is no doubt that acts on both sides, as
necessarily would be the case under such circumstances, *were equally terrible and atrocious.*"*

Observe: though information on particulars was
still wanting, one thing was placed beyond doubt,
the *equality* of guilt and infamy. And I am still,
writing on the 6th of September, dependent mainly
on a foreign source for any official voucher to bring
this testimony to the test. Mr. Schuyler, on the 22nd
of August, reports to the American Government that
the outrages of the Turks were fully established.
He proceeds as follows, with more to the same effect :
" An attempt, however, has been made—and not by
Turks alone—to defend and to palliate them, on the
ground of the previous atrocities which, it is alleged,
were committed by the Bulgarians. I have carefully
investigated this point; and am unable to find that
the Bulgarians committed any outrages or atrocities,
or any acts which deserve that name. *I have vainly
tried to obtain from the Turkish officials a list of such*

---

* 'Times,' July 16.

outrages. . . . . No Turkish women or children were killed in cold blood. No Mussulmen women were violated. No Mussulmans were tortured. No purely Turkish village was attacked or burned. No Mussulman house was pillaged. No mosque was desecrated or destroyed."

The declarations, which had proceeded from the highest authority in the highest Parliamentary Assembly of the world, produced, at the time, an immense effect. They did not remove suspicion, but they effectually baffled and checkmated it, so far as the prevailing sentiment in this country was concerned. So that when, on the 7th of August, the question of cruelties in Bulgaria was yet again raised, a member, and not a young member, " deprecated," says Mr. Ross, in his valuable Record, " party speeches against the Turkish Government."

But it was not only within these shores that the language of the Government was heard. It rang through an astonished Europe. It reached, and it was questioned in, Constantinople. The *Courrier d'Orient* was so bold as to criticise a declaration imputed to the Minister that the alleged burning of the forty girls had been found false upon inquiry instituted. For this offence, in a notice issued by the Director of the Press for Turkey, which I subjoin in the French original, and which referred to the impartiality of the heads of the British Government, and to " *the pretended excesses in Bulgaria* "—note this was on the 9th of August—the journal was suppressed.*

Five attempts had thus been made to penetrate what was still a mystery in the official mind. A sixth and a seventh still followed, on the 9th and the 11th of August. With true British determination, Mr. Ashley opened the question for discussion on the 11th. He was ably supported; and this time, it is pleasant to say, from both sides of the House there

---

*"SUBLIME PORTE.

" MINISTÈRE DES AFFAIRES ÉTRANGÈRES.

" Le Bureau de la Presse,

" Vu le numéro du journal le *Courrier d'Orient* du 8 août :

" Attendu que cette feuille en mentionnant, dans sa revue politique, les déclarations du premier ministre du gouvernement anglais devant le Parlement britannique, (1) touchant les prétendus excès commis en Bulgarie, se fait une sorte de mérite d'avoir été la première à publier la relation de ces crimes supposés ;

" Attendu que la dite feuille se prévaut du silence que la Direction de la presse a gardé à son égard, soit par inadvertence, soit par excès d'indulgence, pour en induire que ses assertions étaient fondées, et que les déclarations du Chef du Cabinet Britannique sont entachées de partialité ;

" Après avoir pris les ordres de S. Exc. le ministre,

" Arrête :

" Le journal le *Courrier d'Orient* est et demeure supprimé à partir du jour de la notification du présent arrêté.

" Constantinople, 9 août, 1876.

" Le Directeur de la Presse,

" BLACQUE."

might be heard the language of humanity, of justice, and of wisdom. It was in the dying throes of the Session. Mr. Ashley's action was especially judicious, because he had a right, which none could contest, to appear as a representative of Lord Palmerston. (The powerful speech of Sir W. Harcourt was denounced by the Prime Minister in terms of great vivacity. He was assured that " from the very commencement of the transactions" the Government "were constantly receiving" from the Ambassador information on " what was occurring in Bulgaria." The Minister selected particular statements for contradiction of details, on which I am not yet sufficiently informed to pronounce ; but what I complain of is that he still, on the 12th of August, effectually disguised the main issue, which lay in the question whether the Turkish Government, which was receiving from us both moral and virtually material support, had or had not by its agents and by its approval and reward of its agents been deeply guilty of excesses, than which none more abominable have disgraced the history of the world. For the Government, it was still merely a question of " civil war," "carried on under conditions of brutality unfortunately not unprecedented in that country," * namely Bulgaria. A repetition of language, which is either that of ignorance, or of brutal calumny upon a people

---

* ' Times,' Aug. 12.

whom Turkish authorities have themselves just described as industrious, primitive, and docile.*

Such then are the steps taken by Her Majesty's Government during the Session with respect to the Bulgarian atrocities, for enlightening the country as some may think, or for keeping it in the dark, as may occur to other and less charitable minds.

It is not the smallest part of the service rendered by the ' Daily News,' that it was probably the means of bringing into the field an American Commission of Inquiry. I have the fullest confidence in the honour and in the intelligence of Mr. Baring, who has been inquiring on behalf of England; because he was chosen for the purpose by Sir H. Elliot, and because I believe he personally well deserves it. But he was not sent to examine the matter until the 19th of July, three months after the rising, and nearly one month after the first inquiries in Parliament. He had been but two days at Philippopolis, when he sent home, with all the dispatch he could use, some few rudiments of a future report. Among them was his estimate of the murders, necessarily far from final, at the figure of twelve thousand.† The leaf, which contains his paper, is almost the only leaf in (the latest) Parliamentary Papers (Turkey, No. 5), " presented to both Houses of Parliament by

---

* In the Report from Philippopolis, to which I shall presently revert.

† Mr. Schuyler's estimate is 15,000 at " the lowest."

Her Majesty's command," which in reference to the main issue is worth more than a straw.* I have read that compilation with pain and humiliation, called forth by finding that this was all which, in the month of August, the whole power and promises of the Government could contribute towards the elucidation of horrible transactions, the greatest and worst of which occurred if not in April, yet early in May. Mr. Baring's Report exists no doubt for us: but only in hope. When it comes, we shall receive it with confidence, and with profit, although we may be very sure that the Ottoman Government will have done everything in its power to blind, and baffle, and mislead him. But is it equally sure, that it will be so received all over Europe? Or, after what has passed, can we reasonably expect that it should? Possibly, when it appears, it may dispute, and even correct, some of the statements now before us. It may establish a few deductions from the awful total. It is one of the painful incidents of a case like this, that injustice may be done unwittingly to this or that man, in this or that circumstance, even by the most necessary and best-considered efforts to attain the ends of justice. These questions do not admit of absolute, but only of reasonable certainty. What seems now to be certain in this sense (besides the miserable daily misgovernment, which, however,

---

* Paper No. 5, p. 5.

dwindles by the side of the Bulgarian horrors) are the wholesale massacres,

> " Murder, most foul as in the best it is,
> But this most foul, strange, and unnatural,"*

the elaborate and refined cruelty—the only refinement of which Turkey boasts!—the utter disregard of sex and age—the abominable and bestial lust—and the utter and violent lawlessness which still stalks over the land. For my own part I have, in the House of Commons and elsewhere, whatever my inward impressions might be, declined to speak strongly on these atrocities, until there was both clear and responsible evidence before me. For want of this evidence, I did not join in the gallant effort of Mr. Ashley, at the last gasp of the Session. But the report of Mr. Schuyler, together with the report from Berlin, and the Prologue, so to call it, of Mr. Baring, in my opinion turns the scale, and makes the responsibility of silence, at least for one who was among the authors of the Crimean War, too great to be borne.

I express then my gratitude to Mr. Schuyler, and to the Government which sent him into the field. It is too late, as I have said, to hope to convince Europe by any report of ours. We may ourselves be sceptical as to Russian reports. Every European State is more or less open to the imputation of bias. But America has neither alliances with Turkey, nor

---

* *Hamlet*, i. 5.

grudges against her, nor purposes to gain by her destruction. She enters into this matter simply on the ground of its broad human character and moment; she has no " American interests " to tempt her from her integrity, and to vitiate her aims.

The ground, then, seemed to be sufficiently laid in point of evidence to call for action, when, as I am writing, a new piece of testimony reaches me* through the courtesy of M. Musurus. It is a French Translation of a Report on the Bulgarian events, dated July 22, presented to the Ottoman Government by a commission of Mussulman and Christian notables, and approved by the Administrative Council of Philippopoli. Since it is put forward as an official statement of the Turkish case (following the Report of Edib Effendi on the 'Vilayet' of Adrianople), I hope it will, for the sake of justice, be extensively read. Others may think differently of it from myself. I cannot but at once denounce it as a disgraceful document; confirmatory, in its moral effect, even of the worst parts of the charges. After all that has happened, it would have been too much to expect a word of penitence or shame; but it does not contain a word of sorrow or compassion. The reporting Commission, which was armed with the powers of the State, wonders that the Bulgarians should have risen against their " paternal "† government; describes them as a

---

* September 2nd.   † P. 17.

peaceable, primitive, and docile people;* and then charges them largely with murdering, burning, impaling, roasting, men, women, and children indiscriminately, with the extremest refinements of cruelty.† One of the most definite statements it contains is this; it cites,‡ as a proof of the "barbarous devastations" committed by the insurgents, the destruction of—a great bridge over the Railway. It is full of laudations of the humanity and consideration of the troops, the commanders, and the Mussulman population.§ It denounces those who have opened the eyes of Europe to this Turkish *Inferno*, as the "fantastic story-makers of dismal episodes." ‖ It takes no notice of the attested fact, that the bodies of slain women and children lie in multitudes, unburied and exposed; except indeed by alleging that at Prestenitza some of the insurgents slew their own women and children. Dated three months after the first outbreak, and full of horrible accusation, it contains hardly in a single instance such verifying particulars as would allow of the detection of falsehood by inquiry into the statement. And it winds up with a particular account of a Pansclavic pamphlet, printed at Moscow in 1867 !

Then, by way of Appendix, comes one original document in proof, which contains, in the form of a sort of Catechism, the plans and instructions of the

---

* Pp. 8, 17.   † Pp. 9, 10.
‡ P. 9.   § E.g. p. 15.   ‖ P. 15.

great Bulgarian conspiracy. They are signed by twelve names of individuals, without profession or employment specified; who may, for all we know, have been the most insignificant men in the country. The Report, however, states that the Insurgents had instructions to massacre the Mussulman population.* The sole document appended in proof of its charges contains, together with very severe provisions against such as should resist, the following passage :†

" *Question* 13. What course is to be pursued with regard to those Turks who submit?

" *Answer*. They should be put in charge of our agents, who will convey them to the headquarters of the insurrection. From thence, they will be sent, with their families and with the aged, to the places occupied for refuge by our own families. *They are to live there as our brethren. It is part of our duty to take care for their happiness, their life, and their religion : on the same ground as for the life and the honour of our own people.*"

The perusal of this statement of the Turkish case removes from my mind any remaining scruple. The facts are, in the gross, sufficiently established. The next, and for us the gravest part of the inquiry is, What have we had to do with them ?

---

* P. 5.   † P. 22.

THE BRITISH FLEET AT BESIKA BAY.

It was on the 20th of April that the insurrection broke out in Bulgaria. In the beginning of May, the horrors of the repression had reached their climax. We had then no other concern in them than this very indirect one, that we were supporting rather too blindly and unwarily in the councils of Europe the supposed interest of the Power, which thus disgraced itself.

On the 9th of May, Sir Henry Elliot seems to have had no consular information about Bulgaria, except a statement (strange enough) from Adrianople, dated the 6th,* that as far as appeared the Turks were not committing any acts of violence against peaceful Christians. But, observing a great Mahomedan excitement, and an extensive purchase of arms in Constantinople, he wisely telegraphed to the British Admiral in the Mediterranean, expressing a desire that he would bring his squadron to Besika Bay. The purpose was, for the protection of British subjects, and of the Christians in general.† This judicious act, done by the Ambassador in conjunction with the Ambassadors of other Powers, who seem to have taken similar steps, was communicated by him to Lord Derby on the 9th of May by letter and by telegraph.‡

On the fifth, had occurred the murder of the French

---

* Parl. Papers, Turkey, No. 3, 1876, p. 145.
† Ibid. p. 146.   ‡ Ibid. p. 129.

and German Consuls at Salonica. On the 15th, the Admiralty acquainted the Foreign Office that the squadron was ordered to Besika Bay, the 'Swiftsure' sent to Salonica, and (as Sir H. Elliot had also asked) the 'Bittern' to Constantinople.‡ These measures, were substantially wise, and purely pacific. They had, if understood rightly, no political aspect; or if any, one rather anti-Turkish than Turkish.

But there were reasons, and strong reasons, why the public should not have been left to grope out for itself the meaning of a step so serious, as the movement of a naval squadron towards a country disturbed both by revolt, and by an outbreak of murderous fanaticism.

In the year 1853, when the negotiations with Russia' had assumed a gloomy and almost a hopeless aspect, the English and French fleets were sent Eastwards: not as a measure of war, but as a measure of preparation for war, and proximate to war. The proceeding marked a transition of discussion into that angry stage, which immediately precedes a blow; and the place, to which the fleets were then sent, was Besika Bay. In the absence of information, how could the British nation avoid supposing that the same act, as that done in 1853, bore also the same meaning?

It is evident that the Foreign Minister was sagaciously alive to this danger. On the 10th of May, he asked Sir H. Elliot for a particular statement of

‡ Parl. Papers, Turkey, No. 3, 1876, p. 147.

THE QUESTION OF THE EAST.

the reasons, which had led him to desire the presence
of the squadron "at Besika Bay." *   He indicated to
the Admiralty Smyrna as a preferable destination.†
And this he actually ordered; but he yielded, and I
believe he was quite right in yielding, to the renewed
and just instances of the Ambassador.

The Government, then, were aware of the purely
pacific character of this measure, and also that it was
one liable to be dangerously misconstrued.

There was another reason for securing it from
misinterpretation. At this very time, the Berlin
Memorandum was prepared. It was announced by
Lord Odo Russell to Lord Derby on May the 13th;
and, on May 15th, he sent to Lord Odo an elaborate
pleading, rather than argument, against it.‡   It be-
came known to the public that we were in diplomatic
discord with Europe, and particularly with Russia.
Now the transition from discussion pure and simple
to discussion backed by display of force is a transition of vast and vital importance. The dispatch of
the fleet to Besika Bay, could not but be interpreted,
in the absence of explanation, as marking that
perilous transition. And yet explanation was re-
solutely withheld.

The expectation of a rupture pervaded the public
mind. The Russian Funds fell very heavily, under
a war panic; partisans exulted in a diplomatic victory,

---

* Parl. Papers, Turkey, No. 3, 1876, p. 130.
† Ibid. p. 131.   ‡ Ibid. pp. 137, 147.

and in the increase of what is called our *prestige*, the bane, in my opinion, of all upright politics. The Turk was encouraged in the humour of resistance. And this, as we now know, while his hands were so reddened with Bulgarian blood. Foreign capitals were amazed at the martial excitement in London. But the Government never spoke a word.

Silence in these circumstances was bad enough. But they were worse than silent. They caused the clang of preparation to be heard in the arsenals. They progressively increased the squadron to a fleet; and, moreover, I believe it is true that they mainly increased it, not by sending the class of ships which had large crews, available for landing considerable numbers of men, for the purpose of defending such persons as might be assailed; but those vast ironclads, with crews relatively small, which principally, and proudly, display the belligerent power of England. If this be not an accurate statement, let it be contradicted.*

And this ostentatious protection to Turkey, this wanton disturbance of Europe, was continued by our Ministry, with what I must call a strange perversity, for weeks and weeks. It was so continued, when a word of explanation as to the true cause of the dispatch of the fleet would have stopped all mischief,

---

* July 27. Mr. Disraeli stated that the Fleet then in Turkish waters consisted of twenty vessels: eleven ironclads, and nine unarmoured ships of war.

dissipated all alarm. I admit, that it would have also dissipated at the same time a little valueless popularity, too dearly bought.

All this time, so far as we can learn, the sequels in detail to the wholesale massacres in Bulgaria were proceeding. In the latter part of it, the fencing answers of the Ministry about Turkish misdeeds had begun. And during the latter part of it also, the requests of members of Parliament for authentic information about the East, were repeatedly refused; on the ground that the production of it would be injurious to the public service! Nay more, compliments were accepted, with the silence which not only might mean consent, but could mean nothing else, from more than one Peer in the House of Lords, and from two members of Parliament in the House of Commons, on the vigorous policy which our Government was pursuing in the East.

Such is the spectacle which, during the present spring and summer, we have exhibited to Europe.

At last came a day of disclosure. Lord Derby received at the Foreign Office, on the 14th of July, a numerous and weighty deputation. They went there in the interests of peace, to which I cordially wish well, and of non-interference—a word which, in my opinion, must be construed, especially for the East of Europe, with a just regard to our honourable engagements, and to the obligations they entail. These gentlemen did not at all approve of the demonstration in Besika Bay. Lord Derby justified it, by admitting that portion of Parliament and the public, who formed the Deputation, for the first time, to the knowledge of the truth. He stated that it was sent, at the request of Sir H. Elliot, for the defence of the Christians against a possible outbreak of Mahometan fanaticism. The country, or great part of it, felt relieved and grateful. But the mischief that had been done by the moral support, and I say boldly by the material support, afforded to Turkey during all those blood-stained weeks (the Servian war, too, was now raging) was not, and could not be, remedied. To repair, in some degree, the effects of that mischief is now a prime part of the peculiar obligation imposed upon the people of this country. For, in fact, whatever our intentions may have been, it is our doing.

And how are we, in this particular, to set about the work of reparation ? Any reader who has accompanied me thus far will probably expect that I, at least, shall answer the question by recommending the withdrawal of the Fleet from Besika Bay. But such, I must at once say, is not my view of duty or of policy. I would neither recall the fleet, nor reduce it by one ship or man.

We have been authoritatively warned, that the condition of the Christians in Turkey is now eminently critical. The issue of the war is still hanging in the balances, which have wavered from day to day. The lapse of time, and possibly aid from without, may still do much to retrieve the vast inequality of chance, with which the brave but raw levies of Servia carry on the contest. We are told, with too much appearance of credibility, that if the fortune of war should veer adversely to Turkey, the consequence might be, in various provinces, a new and wide outbreak of fanaticism, and a wholesale massacre. My hope, therefore, is twofold. First, that, through the energetic attitude of the people of England, their Government may be led to declare distinctly, that it is for purposes of humanity alone that we have a fleet in Turkish waters. Secondly, that that fleet will be so distributed as to enable its force to be most promptly and efficiently applied, in case of need, on Turkish soil, in concert with the other Powers, for the defence of innocent lives, and to prevent the repetition of those recent scenes, at which hell itself might almost blush.

For it must not be forgotten that the last utterance on this subject was from the Prime Minister, and was to the effect that our fleet was in the East for the support of British interests. I object to this constant system of appeal to our selfish leanings. It sets up false lights; it hides the true; it disturbs the world. Who has lifted a finger against British interests ? Who has spoken a word ? If the declaration be anything beyond mere idle brag, it means that our fleet is waiting for the dissolution of the Turkish Empire, to have the first and the strongest hand in the seizure of the spoils. If this be the meaning, it is pure mischief: and if we want to form a just judgment upon it, we have only to put a parallel case. What should we say, if Russia had assembled an army on the Pruth, or Austria on the Danube, and Prince Gortschakoff or Count Andrassy were to announce that it was so gathered, and so posted, for the defence of Russian, or of Austrian interests respectively?

Perhaps, in these unusual circumstances, before describing what it is that we should seek and should desire, it may be well to consider what we should carefully eschew. In the channel, which we have to navigate with or without our Government, there are plenty of false lights set up for us, which lead to certain shipwreck. The matter has become too painfully real for us to be scared at present by the standing hobgoblin of Russia.* Many a time has it done good service on the stage: it is at present out of repair, and unavailable. It is now too late to argue, as was argued sometime back by a very clever and highly enlightened evening Journal, that it might be quite proper that twelve or thirteen millions of Christians in Turkey should remain unhappy, rather than that (such was the alternative hardily pre-

---

* Yet it appears to be considered good enough for the electors of Bucks (I judge from a reported speech of Mr. Fremantle). They seem to be treated, as Railway Companies are sometimes said to treat obscure branch lines, with their worn-out rolling-stock, not presentable in more fashionable districts.

sented) two hundred millions of men in India should be deprived of the benefits of British rule, and thirty millions more in the United Kingdom made uncomfortable by the apprehension of such a catastrophe. But more plausible delusions are about. What we have to guard against is imposture; that Proteus with a thousand forms. A few months ago, the new Sultan served the turn, and very well. Men affirmed that he must have time. And now another new Sultan is in the offing. I suppose it will be argued that he must have time too. Then there will be perhaps new constitutions; firmans of reforms; proclamations to commanders of Turkish armies, enjoining extra humanity. All these should be quietly set down as simply equal to zero. At this moment we hear of the adoption by the Turks of the last and most enlightened rule of warfare ; namely, the Geneva Convention. They might just as well adopt the Vatican Council, or the British Constitution. All these things are not even the oysters before the dinner. Still worse is any plea founded upon any reports made by Turkish authority upon the Bulgarian outrages. This expedient has been long ago tried by sending a Special Commissioner, Edib Effendi, who relates in effect that the outrages were small, and almost all committed by the Christians. Mr. Schuyler, officially, and with an American directness, declares that Edib's report contains statements on a particular point, " *and on every other*, which are utterly unfounded in fact," and that it

practically is " a tissue of falsehoods." Again ; one of
the latest artifices is to separate the question of Servia
from the question of Herzegovina and Bosnia and of
Bulgaria. How, asks the ' Pall Mall Gazette,' can
Turkey improve their condition while war is going
on ? *Inter arma silent leges.* Give her peace, that she
may set about reforms. If the people of this country
are in earnest, they will brush aside all these and all
other cobwebs, and will march as if they marched to
drum and fife, straight, with one heart and one mind,
ohne Hast und ohne Rast, towards their aim.

The case of the Servian war is, in outer form,
quite distinct from that of the misgovernment in
Bosnia and the Herzegovina ; and these again, from
the Bulgarian outrages. But they are distinct simply
as the operations in the Baltic, during the Crimean
War, were distinct from the operations in the Black
Sea. They had one root ; they must surely have one
remedy, I mean morally one ; and administered by
the same handling ; for, if one part of the question be
placed in relief, and one in shadow, the light will not
fall on the dark places, and guilt will gain impunity.

The case against Servia is the best part of the
Turkish case. Servia, before she moved, had suffered
no direct injury ; she had no stateable cause of war.
It does not follow that she has committed a wanton
aggression, or has, in fact, been guilty of any moral
offence. A small and recently ordered State, with a
weak government, and a peninsular territory, she is

surrounded on every side by Sclave populations;
along three-fourths of her frontier, by oppressed and
misgoverned Sclave populations; along nearly half
of it, by a Sclave population in actual revolt, whom
the Turks had been unable to put down, and whom
Europe had ceased, since we succeeded in overthrow-
ing the Berlin Memorandum, actively, though paci-
fically, to befriend. Could her people do otherwise
than sympathise with these populations? Could
they, ought they to have recognised in Turkey an
indefeasible right of oppression? Further, Montenegro, at a very small distance, was throbbing with
emotions similar to her own.

Now there are states of affairs, in which human
sympathy refuses to be confined by the rules, necessarily limited and conventional, of international law.
If any Englishman doubts that such a case may,
though rarely, occur, let him remember the public
excitement of this country nine months ago respecting the Slave Circulars of the Government; and ask
himself whether we model our proceedings towards
slaveholding powers, respecting runaways, on the
precise provisions of international law. Now such a
case did arrive in the position of Servia and Montenegro two months ago. As long as European
action gave a hope of redress for their brethren, peace
was maintained. I hold that in going to war, when
that hope was finally withdrawn, they might plead
human sympathies, broad, deep, and legitimate, and
that they committed no moral offence. Their case

is, therefore, one with that of the oppressed provinces in their neighbourhood. It would have been as reasonable for the Thirteen Colonies of America in 1782, to negotiate separately for peace with Great Britain, as it would be for Europe in 1876 to allow that, in a settlement with Turkey, the five cases of Servia, Bosnia, Herzegovina, Montenegro, and Bulgaria, should be dealt with otherwise than as the connected limbs of one and the same transaction.

There is yet one other danger. Do not let us ask for, do not let us accept, Jonahs or scapegoats, either English or Turkish. It is not a change of men that we want, but a change of measures. New Sultans or ministers among Turks, new consuls or new ambassadors in Turkey, would only in my opinion divert us, at this moment, from the great practical aims in view. Besides, if we are to talk of changing men, the first question that will arise will be that of our Ministers at home, to whose policy and bias both Ministers and subordinate officers abroad always feel a loyal desire as far as may be to conform. In my hope and my opinion, when once the old illusions as to British sentiment are dispelled, and Lord Derby is set free, with his clear, impartial mind and unostentatious character, to shape the course of the Administration, he will both faithfully and firmly give effect to the wishes of the country.

We come now to consider the objects we should desire and seek for through our Government.

I trust they will endeavour to make up, by means of the future, for the serious deficiencies of the past. Let them cast aside their narrow and ill-conceived construction of the ideas of a former period. I am well aware of the necessity which, after the severe labours of the Parliamentary Session, obliges the Ministers to disperse for a period of repose. Nevertheless, in so grave a state of facts, I trust we shall soon hear of a meeting of the Cabinet. It is not yet too late, but it is very urgent, to aim at the accomplishment of three great objects, in addition to the termination of the war, yet (in my view) inseparably associated with it.

1. To put a stop to the anarchical misrule (let the phrase be excused), the plundering, the murdering, which, as we now seem to learn upon sufficient evidence, still desolate Bulgaria.

2. To make effectual provision against the recurrence of the outrages recently perpetrated under the sanction of the Ottoman Government, by excluding its administrative action for the future, not only from Bosnia and the Herzegovine, but also, and above all, from Bulgaria; upon which at best there will remain, for years and for generations, the traces of its foul and bloody hand.

3. To redeem by these measures the honour of the British name, which, in the deplorable

E

events of the year, has been more gravely
compromised than I have known it to be at
any former period.

I have named, then, three great aims, which ought
I think at this crisis to be engraved on the heart, and
demanded by the voice, of Britain. I may be asked,
either seriously or tauntingly, whether there is not
also a fourth to be added, namely, the maintenance
of the " territorial integrity of Turkey."

In order to comprehend the force and bearing of
this expression, it is necessary to go back for a
moment to the Crimean War. The watchword of
that War, and of the policy which preceded it, was
" The integrity and independence of Turkey." Of
these two phrases, integrity and independence, the
bearing is perfectly distinct. The first is negative,
the second positive. The integrity of Turkey will
be maintained by a titular sovereignty, verified as it
were through a moderate payment of tribute, in order
that Ottoman sovereignty may serve the purpose of
shutting out from the present limits of the Turkish
Empire any other sovereignty, or any exercise, in
whole or in part, of sovereign rights by any other
Power, whether it be Russia on the Euxine, or
Austria on the Danube, or France or England on the
Nile and the Red Sea.

The independence of the Ottoman Empire is a very
different affair. It meant at the time of the Crimean

War, and it means now, that, apart from Roumania and Servia, where Europe is already formally concerned, and apart from any arrangements self-made with a vassal State like Egypt, which can hold its own against Constantinople, the Porte is to be left in the actual, daily, and free administration of all the provinces of its vast dominion.

Now, as regards the territorial integrity of Turkey, I for one am still desirous to see it upheld, though I do not say that desire should be treated as of a thing paramount to still higher objects of policy. For of all the objects of policy, in my conviction, humanity, rationally understood, and in due relation to justice, is the first and highest. My belief is that this great aim need not be compromised, and that other important objects would be gained, by maintaining the territorial integrity of Turkey.

There is no reason to suppose that, at the present moment, any of the Continental Powers are governed by selfish or aggressive views in their Eastern Policy. The neighbours of Turkey, namely Austria and Russia, are the two Powers who might, in many conceivable states of European affairs, most naturally be tempted into plans of self-aggrandizement at her expense. But the peculiar conformation of Austria, in respect to territories and to the races which inhabit them, has operated, and will probably at least for the present operate, so as to neutralize this temptation. In the case of Russia, we have been playing, through our

E 2

Government, a game of extreme indiscretion. ， Pretending to thwart, to threaten, and to bully her, we have most mal-adroitly, and most assiduously, played into her hands. Every circumstance of the most obvious prudence dictates to Russia, for the present epoch, what is called the waiting game. Her policy is, to preserve or to restore tranquillity for the present, and to take the chances of the future. We have acted towards her as if she had a present conspiracy in hand, and as if the future did not exist, or never could arrive. But, regard it or not, arrive it will. It offers Russia many chances. One acquisition, if now made by her, would bring those chances very near to certainties. In European Turkey, it cannot too often be repeated, the Christian element is the growing, and the Turkish the decaying one. If a conviction can but be engendered in the Christian, that is for the present purpose mainly the Sclavonic mind of the Turkish provinces, that Russia is their stay, and England their enemy, then indeed the command of Russia over the future of Eastern Europe is assured. And this conviction, through the last six months, we have done everything that was in our power to beget and to confirm.

But we may, I hope, say truly what Louis Napoleon, in 1870, telegraphed in error: *tout peut se rétablir.* Russia has in late years done much to estrange the Greek Christians of the Levant: and the Sclaves will, we may be sure, be at least as ready to accept help from Powers which are perforce more disinterested, as from Powers that may hereafter hope and claim to be repaid for it in political influence or supremacy. It is surely wise, then, to avail ourselves of that happy approach to unanimity which prevails among the Powers, and to avert, or at the very least postpone, as long as we honourably can, the wholesale scramble, which is too likely to follow upon any premature abandonment of the principle of territorial integrity for Turkey. I for one will avoid even the infinitesimal share of responsibility, which alone could now belong to any of my acts or words, for inviting a crisis, of which at this time the dimensions must be large, and may be almost illimitable.

But even that crisis I for one would not agree to avert, or to postpone, at the cost of leaving room for the recurrence of the Bulgarian horrors. Nothing could exceed the mockery, and nothing could redeem the disgrace, of a pretended settlement, which should place it in the power of Turkey to revive these fell Satanic orgies : a disgrace of which the largest share would accrue to England, but of which the smallest share would be large indeed. The public of this country, now I trust awakened from sloth to nobleness, may begin to fear lest the integrity of Turkey should mean immunity for her unbounded savagery, her unbridled and bestial lust. I think these apprehensions, so reasonable in principle, or if there were

ground for them, may be dismissed upon an obser-
vation of the facts.   We have, in the neighbouring
province of Roumania, a testimony which appears to
be nearly conclusive.   For twenty years it has, while
paying tribute to the Porte, and acknowledging
its supremacy, enjoyed an entire autonomy or self-
government.   It has constituted a real barrier for
Turkey against the possibilities of foreign aggression.   It has overcome for itself serious in-
ternal difficulties, in the adjustment of the relations
between class and class.   It has withstood the
temptation to join in the Servian war.   Guaranteed
by Europe, it has had no grave complaint to make
against Turkey for the violation of its stipulated
rights, which have indeed been not inconsiderably
enlarged.   With such an example before us, let us
hope at least that the territorial integrity of Turkey
need not be impaired, while Europe summons and
requires her to adopt the measure which is the very
least that the case demands, namely the total withdrawal of the administrative rule of the Turk from
Bulgaria, as well as, and even more than, from
Herzegovina and from Bosnia.

But even this minimum of satisfaction for the past,
and of security for the future, I am sorrowfully convinced will not be obtained, unless the public voice of
this country shall sound it clearly and loudly, beyond
all chances of mistake, in the ears of the Administration.   We have fortunately obtained a rather recent

disclosure of the purposes of the Government through the mouth of the Prime Minister. On the 31st of July (when we knew so much less than now), after endeavouring to describe the hopeless impotence of the Turkish Government, and to point out that any effectual measures of redress or security must lie in the direction of local self-government for the disturbed provinces, I expressed the hope that this end might be obtained compatibly with the "territorial integrity" of Turkey. The Prime Minister, who followed me in the debate, did me the honour to refer to this portion of my speech, and said I had recommended the re-establishment of the *status quo*. Across the table I at once threw the interjection, "not *status quo*, but territorial integrity." The Prime Minister promptly replied, that territorial integrity would be found virtually to mean the *status quo*. Now the territorial integrity means the retention of a titular supremacy, which serves the purpose of warding off foreign aggression. The *status quo* means the maintenance of Turkish administrative authority in Bosnia, Herzegovina, and Bulgaria. Territorial integrity shuts out the foreign state; the *status quo* shuts out the inhabitants of the country, and keeps (I fear) everything to the Turk, with his airy promises, his disembodied reforms, his ferocious passions, and his daily, gross, and incurable misgovernment. This, then, is the latest present indication of British policy, the re-establishment of the *status quo*. Let us take the phrase out of the dress of the learned language, which somewhat hides its beauty. It means "as you were." It means the re-establishment of the same forms and the same opportunities, which again mean, on the arrival of the first occasion, the same abuses and the same crimes. This purpose of the Government, I feel convinced, is not irrevocable. But it will only be revoked, if we may take experience for our guide, under the distinct and intelligible action of public opinion. No man will so well understand as the Prime Minister what is the force and weight of that opinion; and at what stage, in the development of a national movement, its expression should no longer be resisted.

Since the ominous declaration of Lord Beaconsfield on the *status quo*, or "as you were" policy, there has appeared a letter from Mr. Bourke, the Under-Secretary of the Foreign Office; which could not have been written without higher sanction. Of this letter, the positive part is null, the negative part important. It assures us of the indignation of the Government at the crimes committed by the Turks. It might as well assure us of their indignation at the crimes of Danton, or of Robespierre, or of Nana Sahib. Indignation is froth, except as it leads to action. This indignation has led, he says, to remonstrance. I say that mere remonstrance, in this case, is mockery. The only two things that are worth saying, the Under-Secretary does not say. The first of them would have been that, until these horrible outrages are redressed, and their authors punished, the British

Government would withdraw from Turkey the moral and even material support we have been lending her against Europe. The other was, that after crimes of so vast a scale and so deep a dye, the British Government would no longer be a party to the maintenance of Turkish administration in Bulgaria. It is, then, the negative part of this letter that signifies. Mr. Bourke's words, viewing their date, are futile. But his silence is trumpet-tongued: it proclaims that even last week, on the 27th of August, the Government were still unconverted; and, warning us what we have to expect, it spurs the people of England onwards in the movement, which is to redeem its compromised and endangered honour.

It would not be practicable, even if it were honourable, to disguise the real character of what we want from the Government. It is a change of attitude and policy, nothing less. We want them to undo and efface that too just impression, which, while keeping their own countrymen so much in the dark, they have succeeded in propagating throughout Europe, that we are the determined supporters of the Turk, and that, declaring his "integrity and independence" essential to "British interests," we have winked hard, and shall wink, if such be, harder still, according to the exigencies of the case, alike at his crimes and at his impotence. We want to place ourselves in harmony with the general sentiment of civilized mankind, instead of being any longer, as

we seem to be, the Evil Genius which dogs, and
mars, and baffles it. We want to make the Turk
understand that, in conveying this impression by
word and act to his mind, the British Government
have misunderstood, and, therefore, have misrepre-
sented, the sense of the British people.

But this change is dependent on an emphatic
expression of the national sentiment, which is but
beginning to be heard. It has grown from a whisper
to a sound; it will grow from a sound to a peal.
But what, *until* it shall vibrate with such force as to
awaken the Administration ? It is melancholy, but
it is also true, that we, who upon this Eastern
ground fought with Russia, and thought Austria
slack, and Germany all but servile, have actually for
months past been indebted, and are even now indebted, to all or some of these very Powers, possibly to
Russia most among them, for having played the part
which we think specially our own, in resistance to
tyranny, in befriending the oppressed, in labouring
for the happiness of mankind. I say the time has
come for us to emulate Russia by sharing in her
good deeds, and to reserve our opposition until she
shall visibly endeavour to turn them to evil account.

There is no reason to apprehend serious difficulty
in the Councils of Europe on this subject. All the
Powers, except ourselves, have already been working
in this direction. Nor is there any ground to suppose
that the Ottoman Government will tenaciously resist a

scheme based on the intention to do all in its favour that its own misconduct, and the fearful crimes of its trusted agents, have left possible. To do this Government justice, a distinction must be drawn between what depends upon a decision to be taken at Constantinople once for all, and the permanent vitalizing force required for the discharge of the daily duties of administration all over its vast empire. The central agency at the capital, always under the eye of the representatives of the European Powers and in close contact with them, has acquired, and traditionally transmits, a good deal of the modes of European speech and thought. It is when they try to convey these influences to the provinces and the subordinate agents, who share little or none of that beneficial contact and supervision, that they, except here and there by some happy accident of personal virtue, habitually and miserably break down. The promises of a Turkish Ministry given simply to Europe are generally good; those given to its own subjects or concerning its own affairs are, without imputing absolute mendacity, of such tried and demonstrated worthlessness, that any Ambassador or any State, who should trust them, must come under suspicion of nothing less than fraud by wilful connivance. The engagement of a Turkish Ministry, taken in concert with Europe, that Bulgaria, or any other province, shall now settle and hereafter conduct its own local government and affairs, would carry within itself the guarantee of its own execution. The only question is, whether it would be given or withheld. I am disposed to believe it would be given, not withheld; and for this reason. I know of no case in which Turkey has refused to accede to the counsel of United Europe, nay, even of less than United Europe, if Europe was not in actual schism with itself under unwise or factious influences. In the matter of Greece, in the Union of the Principalities after the Crimean War, and in the conduct of its relations (for example) with Persia and with Egypt, there has been abundant proof that the Ottoman Porte is no more disposed than other governments, in the homely phrase, to drive its head against a brick wall. It has known how to yield, not ungracefully, to real necessity, without provoking violence. And those of its self-constituted friends, who warn us against an outburst of wild Mohammedan fanaticism within the Cabinet of Constantinople, and in the year 1876, found themselves on notions drawn from their own fancy, or from what they call having been in the East, much more than on the recorded lessons of political and diplomatic experience.

No doubt there will be difficulties to overcome when these provinces set about their own affairs, in adjusting relations with the Mahometan minorities. These are difficulties insurmountable to those who have not the will to surmount them, but easily surmounted under the real pressure of such a case. They were sur-

mounted in Greece; and at this hour, as we learn by
the very recent testimony of Sir Charles Trevelyan,
Mahometan landlords in Eubœa live contentedly under
the Government of that country. Mahometan, it
must be remembered, does not mean the same as Turk.
And in none of these provinces has it been in the main
a case of war between conflicting religions or local
races: nearly the whole mischief has lain in the
wretched laws, and the agents at once violent and cor-
rupt, of a distant central Power, which (having none
others) lets these agents loose upon its territory; and
which has always physical force at its command to back
outrage with the sanction of authority, but has no
moral force whatever, no power either of checking
evil or of doing good.

But I return to, and I end with, that which is the
Omega as well as the Alpha of this great and most
mournful case. An old servant of the Crown and
State, I entreat my countrymen, upon whom far
more than perhaps any other people of Europe it
depends, to require, and to insist, that our Government, which has been working in one direction, shall
work in the other, and shall apply all its vigour to
concur with the other States of Europe in obtaining
the extinction of the Turkish executive power in
Bulgaria. Let the Turks now carry away their abuses
in the only possible manner, namely by carrying off
themselves. Their Zaptiehs and their Mudirs, their
Bimbashis and their Yuzbachis, their Kaimakams and

their Pashas, one and all, bag and baggage, shall, I hope, clear out from the province they have desolated and profaned. This thorough riddance, this most blessed deliverance, is the only reparation we can make to the memory of those heaps on heaps of dead; to the violated purity alike of matron, of maiden, and of child; to the civilization which has been affronted and shamed; to the laws of God or, if you like, of Allah; to the moral sense of mankind at large. There is not a criminal in an European gaol, there is not a cannibal in the South Sea Islands, whose indignation would not rise and overboil at the recital of that which has been done, which has too late been examined, but which remains unavenged; which has left behind all the foul and all the fierce passions that produced it, and which may again spring up, in another murderous harvest, from the soil soaked and reeking with blood, and in the air tainted with every imaginable deed of crime and shame. That such things should be done once, is a damning disgrace to the portion of our race which did them; that a door should be left open for their ever-so-barely possible repetition would spread that shame over the whole. Better, we may justly tell the Sultan, almost any inconvenience, difficulty, or loss associated with Bulgaria,

> "Than thou reseated in thy place of light,
> The mockery of thy people, and their bane."*

---

* Tennyson's 'Guinevere.'

We may ransack the annals of the world, but I know not what research can furnish us with so portentous an example of the fiendish misuse of the powers established by God " for the punishment of evil-doers, and for the encouragement of them that do well." No Government ever has so sinned; none has so proved itself incorrigible in sin, or which is the same, so impotent for reformation. If it be allowable that the Executive power of Turkey should renew at this great crisis, by permission or authority of Europe, the charter of its existence in Bulgaria, then there is not on record, since the beginnings of political society, a protest that man has lodged against intolerable misgovernment, or a stroke he has dealt at loathsome tyranny, that ought not henceforward to be branded as a crime.

But we have not yet fallen to so low a depth of degradation; and it may cheerfully be hoped that, before many weeks have passed, the wise and energetic counsels of the Powers, again united, may have begun to afford relief to the overcharged emotion of a shuddering world.

Having done with the argumentative portion of the case, I desire to perform yet one other duty, by reminding my countrymen that measures appear to be most urgently required for the relief of want, disease, and every form of suffering in Bulgaria.

Lady Strangford has, with energetic benevolence, proposed to undertake this work. It seems to me to go far beyond the powers of any individual, however active and intelligent. I will presume to urge that, under the peculiar circumstances of the case, there is a call upon Her Majesty's Government to take the matter in hand. I do not mean by means of a grant of public money: but by communicating with the municipal and local authorities, and submitting to them the expediency of opening subscriptions: by placing the whole machinery of the Embassy at Constantinople and of the Consulates and Vice-Consulates at the service of the undertaking; and by supplying men able to organize and superintend the distribution of relief from the military and possibly also the naval departments.

HAWARDEN, CHESTER,
　5th Sept., 1876.

LONDON: PRINTED BY WILLIAM CLOWES AND SONS, STAMFORD STREET
AND CHARING CROSS.

www.ingramcontent.com/pod-product-compliance
Lightning Source LLC
Chambersburg PA
CBHW031243260626
47169CB00007B/2426